Heaven's Bell

By
Sherrie Barch

I wasn't quite sure what to expect as I started reading this book but as I started to read it, I could not put it down! It is such a beautiful and comforting way to view what happens after we pass from this life. It is a book that is an easy read and a message that is very relevant for children and adults. *Heaven's Bell* gives the reader an appreciation for both life and death in a most grateful way.

—Heidi B.

This is a compassionate look at death from a new author who understands children and creates a beautiful story of friendship and loss, with hope and comfort. A great read for any young person who has lost someone, or even someone who has not yet had that experience, but will face it in the future. The book says it is geared towards 8-12 year-olds, and that seems just right, although as an adult I enjoyed it too.

—Amazon Reviewer

The author does such a fantastic job of creating a space, both within these pages and in your mind, that affords you the opportunity to believe that the story of life ends happily. The book is highly relatable and comforting. It is also clever in its positioning of that part of life that is often with challenge; the loss of a loved one. It welcomes you into a place of respite.

—Scott L.

We all need hope; and we all need to know things will (eventually) be ok. This book will help children and adults find the hope they so desperately need in bereavement. I especially loved that the author included her "Original Story" which inspired the book.

—Gloria P.

Editor: Elizabeth Carson, thebethcarson@gmail.com

Project Management: Shannon Rhea, www.creativeapogee.com

Cover & Illustrations: Sabrina Peregolise Telis

Inside Layout: Ljiljana Pavkov, www.bookwormsdesign.com

Printed in the United States of America

FIRST EDITION

Library of Congress

ISBN: 978-1-7362638-0-8

Library of Congress Pending

www.heavensbell.com

For Ron

Acknowledgements

Thank you …

Beth Carson for your early enthusiastic feedback and your editing expertise.

Shannon Rhea for sharing your personal story and patiently showing me how this book will show up in the real world.

Sabrina Peregolise Telis for your help telling this story with your expressive and perfect drawings.

Christine Whitmarsh for picking up this diamond in the rough story and making it shine when this world needed it most!

Brooke for sharing your gifts of inspiration, reflection, and grit with me.

Norm for telling me I could help others with my story and to go for it.

Kim and Elle for believing in this story through the long nights and show and tells.

Paul and Nancy for embracing this story as we all celebrated your son Matt and found peace in the angel clouds.

Chuck, Glo, Gina and Phil for your friendship, encouragement and sharing Lake Castle Rock where *Heaven's Bell* was first penned.

Stacy for your confidence in my ability to story tell.

Edie, Marlene, and Julie for being my inspiring soul sisters who always make time for my stories.

Scott, Jen, Kallie, and Lexi for listening to my very first *Heaven's Bell* stories and as a result, filling us all up with your memories and reflections about Carol.

My loved ones in heaven who I will someday hang bells with and hug in the Great Hall.

My mother for always creating an authentic space for real discussions about life's hard bumps and modeling how to love unconditionally.

Ron, Mitchell, Michael, and Harrison for your perfect and pure love.

Contents

Heaven's
Bell

Letter to Parents

Dear fellow parents:

Thank you for reading my very first children's book, *Heaven's Bell*! The story of BFFs (literally!) Ashley and Cody is based on my short story of the same name you will later get to see in the conclusion.

Being the mother of three boys, two of whom have Type 1 Diabetes, and both diagnosed within one year of each other, Cody's story in particular was an emotional one to write. My sons were diagnosed with Type I Diabetes at the ages of 11 and 7 (they are now 22 and 19).

As a parent you're, of course, trying to do the best you can in that situation, even as the waves of vulnerability and powerlessness washing over you can feel overwhelming. I hope this book offers you a safe window of opportunity to talk about sensitive subjects like illness, chronic illness, pain, and life and death with your family, no matter which health challenges your family may or may not have faced or be facing.

For those parents out there who, like Cody's family in this story, have lost a child - my heart absolutely breaks for you and you have all the thoughts, prayers, and love that I can muster. I truly hope that Cody's story offers even a microscopic piece of healing, which was one of my intentions from day one of this project.

This story is written primarily for kids between the ages of 8 and 12 years old. However, as with all stories, there will undoubtedly be readers outside this age range (even adults!) who find enjoyment, inspiration, and hopefully valuable ideas to explore about life and death. At its core, *Heaven's Bell* is about how Cody's illness and then untimely death impacted those around him, specifically his best friend from kindergarten, Ashley. From the moment they came into being, it was clear these two had one of those special, once-in-a-lifetime friendships that only the luckiest amongst us ever get to experience. It was truly my honor to create them and share their story.

As you and your child read and then discuss Cody and Ashley's story together, here are some things to keep in mind in regards to how children in this age group (8-12 year olds) understand and process death:

- On the younger end of the spectrum children might associate death with old age so this story should be a gentle opportunity to broaden that conversation. Children on the older end of the range understand that death is final and is a certainty for everyone of all ages including themselves.
- Young children may feel fear around death, associating it with things like scary ghosts and spirits in cartoons, while children on the older end of our spectrum demonstrate more complete, "adult" emotions like anger, sadness, and sometimes guilt, shame, and anxiety.
- Children across this age spectrum may experience feelings of insecurity and abandonment, acting out those feelings via behavior issues at school or in social situations, or through physical health symptoms.

- Similar to how Ashley handled Cody's death, older children will understand the impact of a loved one's death on others, and might even be hesitant to display their own emotions, hiding them to "appear strong" around others (like Cody's family).
- Also paralleling Ashley's reaction to the news of Cody's illness, kids of this age may attempt to avoid "heavy" conversations, and quickly flee to the safety of an activity that feels normal (like scrolling on their phone) as soon as possible. Some parents may interpret this as their child not hearing the bad news, but that's usually not the case. Experts recommend that in this situation the parents give their child space and then gently join them in the activity to be there for them when they do have questions or when emotions bubble up.

One of my goals in writing this book was to create a safe space for you and your family to have a conversation about death and dying in a way that feels natural and productive. Above all, the experience I hope you and your child will have in reading this book is one of joy, inspiration, gratitude, and an appreciation of heaven ("outer space") through Ashley and Cody's respective eyes.

As a side note, I wrote this book and am writing this letter to you in the fall of 2020, during one of the most challenging years any of us has faced in our collective lifetime. The COVID-19 pandemic has brought to the forefront the fragility of life and reality of death in people of all ages, all health conditions, and from all walks of life. Children around the world have had to suddenly cope with the deaths of parents, grandparents, siblings, relatives they barely knew, friends, teachers, and schoolmates. In a sense, I have tasked Ashley and Cody with serving as angel guides for you and your family. Consider them your own make- believe friends who temporarily parted on earth but later reunited in heaven.

No matter what your particular religious beliefs or view on death and the afterlife, this story is meant to bring you comfort and hope, wrapped in a shell of smiles and entertainment. In a year like this - we sure need it!

Much Love,
Sherrie Barch

1
Under the Stars

"Are you trying to ditch me???"

Ashley glared at Cody, her long skinny fingers planted on two nearly nonexistent hips, green eyes flashing.

"Ash, no," her BFF said with an exasperated sigh that made him seem older than his 11 years, "I was just saying why don't you at least go over and say hi to Aiden and those guys?"

Carrying his meal tray with one hand, he gestured with his free one across the science museum cafeteria at a bunch of super chatty girls clustered around a small round table.

Ashley thought they looked like hyenas at feeding time, tearing into paper wrapped burgers and little red and white checkered baskets of fries while alternately screeching with laughter, no doubt at weirdly unfunny things.

"First of all," Ashley retorted, "those are not guys, they're all GIRLS," placing emphasis on "girls" as if it were a cuss word.

Cody spotted an empty table and started walking toward it with Ashley following, still ranting.

"Coh, you know what that means..."

Cody placed his tray on the table and plopped down into a chair with another sigh, this time sounding more tired than annoyed.

"Okay, I'll give, what does it mean?" he asked her with a playful smirk.

"Drah-ma!" Ashley exclaimed dramatically as she sat down in the chair across from him, grinning.

"Okay, fine," Cody said with yet another sigh, picking at his lunch unenthusiastically.

Ashley picked up on the sighs and bit her lip nervously but kept quiet, even as the gears in her overactive mind cranked into high gear.

What the heck? Why is Cody suddenly trying to ditch me by getting me to have lunch with Aiden and McKayla and - ugh - Sofie?

None of those girls had anything in common with her. Even the stuff they found funny was weird and random - like the YouTube videos where you're supposed to try not to laugh even though the video is really funny. Of course, that was never a problem for Ashley since she never found the videos really funny - at all!

All day, even before lunch, Cody had been acting bored and tired. Yeah, it was the same science museum field trip they'd been going on since the 1st grade and looking at it all for the sixth time does get boring...

But still.

Ashley bit her lip again and stared across the table at her best friend - really more like a brother, a sibling she'd never had. She studied the face she'd seen most every day of her life since kindergarten. She'd always thought Cody's thin black perfectly straight hair had a calming, organized effect, making him seem like he always had it together even when he was being a goofball (which was a lot). That, along with his dimples, made him look like an angelic vampire. Her own chestnut brown hair, by contrast, seemed to be fighting a constant battle between curling sideways, frizzing up, and lying on her head like a dead cat, which is why she almost always wore it pulled tightly back in a ponytail so she wouldn't have to deal with it- which also worked better for basketball.

Lately though, Cody was taking his unique look to extremes. The dimples seemed to be caving into his increasingly pale face and his dramatic black hair seemed to be thinning. Although, Ashley thought as she finally dug into her own lunch, this might all be her imagination. She was aware of how she tended to exaggerate things to make them more exciting. Her mother regularly pointed this out to her as more of a criticism. Her father, on the other hand, said it was a sign of an active imagination and saw it as a positive. Ashley decided long ago that, of the two, her father was right. She'd already started daydreaming about which careers require an active imagination.

Ten minutes of awkward silence later, Ashley's worrying about why Cody was being weird was rudely interrupted by Mr. Fisher, the cute, new, science teacher who was standing amidst the cluster of tables assigned to Henninger Middle School in Barrington, Illinois.

"Okay people, take your last bites, throw away and recycle, return your trays and gather in your assigned pods over here in the corner. Planetarium show starts in 15 minutes," he announced, clapping his hands together for emphasis.

Ashley looked over at most of the food still sitting on Cody's plate.

"Hey - seriously - what's up?" she asked rather impatiently now. She tried to meet his familiar dark eyes that seemed to be spacing out in the distance.

"Nothing Ash, I'm just tired," Cody said, smiling to reassure her. "C'mon let's go chill out under the STARRRZZZ" he joked as he imitated the announcer guy in the planetarium show.

Ashley laughed and playfully punched him in the shoulder, feeling relieved.

She grabbed both their meal trays and emptied them into nearby bins.

See, that's what the Drama Girls will never understand, she mused.

They saw field trips as an excuse to have the same dumb conversations in a different location. She and Cody treated these days as adventures, something special. This was always their favorite part too, the 'Under the Stars' show they'd both seen a zillion times but still loved.

First they would settle into those same old dingy but awesomely comfy recliner seats, staring up at outer space, even though they both knew it was the old water-stained ceiling of the Chicago Metro Science Museum, with spotlights and laser beams flashing across it. In their imaginations, Ashley and Cody were in outer space. Then, the same announcer guy from forever would give an overly dramatic speech about "The beginning of TIME!" Ashley and Cody would quietly mimic him and burst into laughter.

Then, the show would start and they'd both get sucked into the experience instantly, usually more so than anyone in the room. For about an hour, the rest of the world would disappear as they pretended to be flying through outer space, discovering new worlds together. For that one hour it was the Ash and Coh show.

But now, Ashley's wound-up brain was still nagging at her about Cody's behavior, not just today, but for weeks now. It seemed like they weren't spending as much time together suddenly - fewer games of one-on-one in her driveway, and more and more days where he would disappear before the end of the school day and leave her to bike home alone. Overall, they didn't seem to be having as much fun together anymore.

Ashley hated to admit it, but she was suspicious and even a little mad at the thought that he might have a new best friend and might be slowly pushing her away (especially since at lunch, just now, he tried to push her away to the Drama Girls!). She was constantly racking her brain for clues - had she done something to annoy him?

Nothing more than usual, she thought, fully realizing how obnoxious she could be sometimes. She made a mental promise to herself to maybe tone down "The Ash Show" a little and see if that would make Cody stop acting weird.

Or maybe he had outgrown having a girl as a best friend. The thought of suddenly having to figure out life without her best friend made Ashley's stomach feel queasy (or maybe it was the greasy cheeseburger she'd just wolfed down in, like, four bites).

Or, she thought, as they zoomed past Venus, deeper and deeper into space, maybe Coh was telling her the truth - maybe he *was* just tired.

An hour later, when the lights came back up, Ashley looked over at Cody and laughed at how silly she had been for worrying. Sure enough, in the dingy orange recliner to her left, there was her raven-haired best friend from down the street, fast asleep.

For the time being it seemed like Cody was telling the truth. He was just tired and their friendship was safe.

And more importantly, I won't have to be friends with the Drah-ma Girls!

2
One on One

"FOUL! Flagrant and also completely crazy personal foul!" Cody called out, making a "T" with his hands.

He motioned for Ashley to throw him the basketball.

"No way, I saw MJ do it a hundred times, it's totally legal!" Ashley protested. She pushed some stray sweaty strands of hair behind her ears and blotted her face with her oversized, vintage, Jordan jersey.

"HA!" Cody said, actually laughing out loud at Ashley's lame attempt to make the game go her way, as usual.

He felt winded so he took a seat on a decorative iron bench to the side of Ashley's driveway holding the ball tightly in his lap to keep it away from her.

"If the G.O.A.T. (greatest of all time) ever did anything close to that Ash, then what you just did was a lousy imitation. You elbowed me in the jaw!" Cody said, rubbing his face to make his point.

"You're such a baby sometimes, Coh! It was just a reverse layup - your giant baby face got in the way. Anyway, c'mon and get your butt back here, there's still a lot of game to be played."

Realizing it was pointless to argue with Ashley in the heat of competition, Cody got up, dribbling the ball as he walked back to her on the driveway court.

"What's the score?" he asked, then quickly added, "And don't lie!"

"32-30, me. Go!" Ashley barked, and immediately moved into a guard position in front of Cody.

He sprung into motion, zig zagging nimbly around the driveway with Ashley covering him closely. Finally, unable to get past her and close enough to the hoop for a two pointer, he positioned himself on the edge of the driveway in three point land, raised the ball over his head, sucked in his breath, and took his shot.

SWISH!

"Yeah!" Cody celebrated, pumping his fist in the air and running around the driveway in his own one man victory parade.

Ashley walked to the end of the driveway toward the street, rolled her eyes, and checked her smart watch, pretending to be suddenly bored by the game and fascinated by something on the screen.

"C'mon let's go!" Cody said, still riding his victory high.

"What's the point?" Ashley demanded, still pretending to be more interested in her watch.

"Oh I dunno - the GAME maybe?" Cody said, getting annoyed at his best friend's over-the-top competitiveness. "The point is the game, Ash, always has been... you know that. The game is right even when everything else about the world is going wrong."

Okay, that's a pretty deep thought for a game of one on one!

He jogged up the driveway and extended his arm up to wrap around her shoulder.

"Even when you're losing, it's awesome," Cody said with a flash of excitement in his eye that Ashley hadn't seen in forever. She tried to hide the little smile that formed on her lips but Cody noticed and elbowed her in the side.

"C'mon, let's make MJ proud," he persuaded, grabbing her hand and pulling her back toward the basket.

Just then, a group of boys walking down the sidewalk paused at the end of her driveway, gathering in a lopsided semi-circle.

"Hey Co-KOH!" the lead boy taunted.

Ashley recognized them from school - knuckleheads, all of them. But unfortunately they didn't know this about themselves. They thought they ran the school.

"What're you and your *girl*-friend doing?" the boy continued, pointing at Ashley.

The boys with him played along, chuckling even though nothing was funny.

"What does it look like we're doing, guys?" Cody said conversationally, sounding more like a teacher than a kid their own age.

"It looks like you're both acting like an old, boring, married couple!" one of the boys said, setting off a wave of laughter across the awkward semi-circle.

"Is that what you really think we're doing?" Cody asked seriously, staring them down.

The lead bully puffed out his chest and took a step forward but Cody didn't flinch.

Ashley was puzzled by this new side of her BFF today - first standing up to her over the game, and now standing up to these idiots? She'd never seen him stand up to anyone ever. Cody thought fighting was a waste of time.

Ashley stood watching, curious as to what exactly was about to happen. There was another part of her though, that felt like she should have his back; that she should throw her body in front of Cody's, arms spread out wide to protect him. But for some reason her legs refused to move. So, she just stood and watched.

As it turned out, Cody had his own back.

"Do you guys need something?" Cody said, still not flinching. He simply held the lead boy's gaze with a serene look on his face.

The bully shifted his weight back and forth between his legs doing his best to avoid Cody's gaze. The other boys were at a loss for what to do next, shooting glances at each other and shrugging. One mouthed to the other, *I dunno!* They'd obviously come to pick a fight but were confused that Cody wasn't giving them one.

Ashley watched with curiosity.

"Anyway, we're going to go back to our game now," Cody announced, but not moving, and still staring.

The lead boy came back to life.

"That's all you and your *girl*-friend ever do - play basketball and talk about some dude who played the game like a million years ago," he said with a smirk.

"Yeah, I mean, Michael Jordan - like history much?" one of them chimed in.

"Yes," Cody said matter of factly, "We do like history much. What's the matter with that? What's the big deal about Ash and I liking the best basketball player ever and shooting hoops?"

The lead boy opened his mouth to say something but then closed it, waving his hand with a "whatever." He turned and walked away, his followers trailing behind. But once they were a safe distance away, the boy suddenly stopped, stooped down, picked up a rock from the ground, and lobbed it in their direction.

"Losers!" he yelled.

The rock missed them by the length of a car.

"Maybe that's why they hate us so much," Cody said, turning around with a triumphant grin, "cuz that throw SUCKED!"

He crossed his arms over his chest looking extremely proud of himself, like an early explorer who'd just discovered a new land.

"Well, what did you think?" he asked, looking around for the basketball, still with a smile on his face.

The moment he turned back to face Ashley though, he saw she was mad!

"Why'd you have to do that?????" Ashley screamed furiously.

"Do what? What the heck, Ash?" Cody stammered, trying to figure out what was happening.

"Why did you have to start something with them?" she fumed.

"Oh, I don't know, maybe to stand up for you... for us." Cody said, still confused.

"Who asked you to do that?" the fuming gazelle in front of him asked.

She scrambled to retrieve the ball from the side of the driveway and dribbled it extra hard in the other direction, smashing it into the asphalt harder and harder with every bounce.

"What is the matter with you?" Cody asked.

"Nobody asked you to do that," Ashley grumbled. To avoid looking at him, she took shots at the basket - really bad ones. Mostly airballs. "And now," she continued, finally making her shot, "You've just made everything worse."

"Made what worse?" Cody stammered in disbelief, still trying to understand her.

To squash the sudden urge he felt to run out of her driveway and never come back, Cody grabbed one of Ashley's rebounds and took his own shot - swish! He smiled briefly before remembering he was mad.

Now Ashley grabbed the basketball and hugged it to her chest, forcing Cody to pay attention to her.

"Those guys already treat me like a total freak because I don't act like normal girls - the Drama Girls. Now, you've just made them think about me more, which means they'll hate me more because they're gonna think I'm some freak like you!" she unloaded.

Ashley felt terrible immediately. Cody looked more hurt than when she'd actually screamed at him a couple minutes ago. But unfortunately, her mouth didn't get the message to shut up and all of her recent worries about their friendship poured out.

"And what if, someday, I don't know, you suddenly decide you don't want to be friends with me anymore, and that you'd rather have guy friends because this is weird. The girls already hate me and now the guys hate me too. I'll be all alone - and you SUCK Cody!" Ashley dug her fingernails into the basketball trying to hold it together.

"So, yeah," she said under her breath, "your whole tough guy thing just now didn't do me any favors."

She finally stopped talking and looked up at him, tears welling in her eyes, hoping he might scream at her. At least then it would be a fair fight.

But he didn't. He just stared back at her with that same creepy look he'd used against the lead boy.

"Screw you," she said. She threw the ball back at him and ran inside her house.

Cody laid the basketball carefully down on the bench.

"I wasn't being a tough guy - I was being freakin' Gandhi!" he yelled as he walked back down the driveway toward the sidewalk.

3
Bubble Girl

"Honey, can you come down here please?"

Ashley looked away from her computer and toward the sound of her mother's voice coming from the living room. She bit her lip and sat for a minute. She knew exactly what this was about.

Stalling, she took her time logging out of her school's homework system, leaned back in her desk chair and paused.

"Coming!" she called but she still didn't move.

Ashley replayed the events of the day in her head. It all began (and was entirely caused by, in her opinion) when Cody didn't go to school today.

That in itself was no big deal. She and Cody knew for a fact that adults took sick days from their jobs every now and then - "mental health days" her mother called them. Once they caught onto this, she and Cody didn't think twice about following their lead once in a while - even if faking symptoms was sometimes required.

Ashley naturally assumed that's what Cody did today, especially after their encounter with the bullies the other day. It had been tense since then, between Cody and the boys at school, and she could see how he might need a mental health day.

Truthfully, Ashley felt a little relieved not to have to face him. She and Cody had been polite to each other, but hadn't really talked since the blow up that day. She needed some more time to figure out the right way to apologize for what Cody would probably call her "crazy girl meltdown."

She hadn't meant to say all those hurtful things, but all the worrying about their friendship had been boiling up for months now. Something was bound to blow sooner or later.

In a way, she thought, it was partly his fault. If he hadn't been acting so weird around her lately, she wouldn't have been forced to call him out.

"Ash!" now it was her dad calling up the stairs.

"I KNOW, I'm COMING! I just have to finish this one assignment - the teacher is literally waiting for me to hit send!" she lied at the top of her voice.

So, that was the upside to Cody faking sick and staying home from school today - not having to deal with him. The downside was having to deal with everyone else. Usually this wasn't an issue, she'd just keep her head down and avoid everyone, and everyone would avoid her right back.

Today though, especially without Cody as a buffer, it was like she had a target on her back. As she had suspected, and even *told* Cody it would happen, the bully boys got together with the Drama Girls and decided to gang up on Ashley, since in their eyes, she was a "co-freak." After a day of general glares shot in her direction, behind-the-back laughter at her expense, and kids brushing by her in the hallway hard enough to knock her off balance, it all came to a head in gym class.

As much as Ashley loved basketball, the other "ball" sports - not so much. That day in class they were playing her least favorite sport of all - volleyball. First, it killed her hands. Second, it required talking to, and cooperating with, people she didn't like. And third, for some reason, her head was frequently the target of volleyballs gone wild.

The "incident" happened when Ashley, her competitive juices kicking in and getting the best of her, dove head-first toward a pass. Fingers interlaced tightly with thumbs on top, she fully believed she would make contact with the ball, volley it over the net, and be the hero of third period gym.

Instead, she leapt forward, somehow tripped over her own left foot, careened sideways and came crashing down on top of petite little Aiden - who was *not* happy with this at all!

"Get off me, freak!" Aiden yelled with disgust. She tried to extricate her tiny, perfectly proportioned body from underneath Ashley's freakishly long arms and legs while avoiding the droplets of sweat coming off of Ashley's hair.

Ashley was finally able to roll off Aiden and both girls scrambled to their feet.

"Okay girls, it's red team serve!" Mrs. Jenkins called out from the sidelines and blew her whistle.

"Actually Mrs. J," Aiden called back, "I think I twisted my ankle." She stared at Ashley with a slight smirk.

Oh you have GOT to be kidding me!

"Or more specifically, a certain *someone* twisted her ankle," McKayla chimed in helpfully as the gym teacher walked over.

Ashley stood waiting and fuming, absorbing the heat of the glares coming at her from all the Drama Girls at once. She could feel her face burn deep red and her sweaty hair just kept getting grosser. She wished the floor would open up and swallow her whole.

As Mrs. Jenkins stooped down and checked on Aiden's ankle, Ashley physically couldn't survive the tension that had been building for days, a moment longer.

"I did NOT twist your stupid ankle!" she screamed like a screeching teapot.

Then, not waiting to see how it would all play out, she fled across the gym and back to the locker room, spending the rest of gym class hiding in a cold shower, letting the stream of water wash away her tears and mat her sweaty hair to her scalp like a helmet. She wanted to talk to Cody so bad and make things normal again.

As the shower water poured down, Ashley pictured a giant bubble forming around her, separating her from the real world. The walls of the bubble began to blur her surroundings and she felt herself calming down. But Ashley's escape fantasy was rudely interrupted by shrieks of laughter from her classmates entering the locker room. She sighed as the bubble dissolved into the shower stream.

Now back home sitting at her desk, she gazed distractedly at the late afternoon orange rays of sun hitting the mostly sports posters on her wall. The orange tinted streaks made Michael Jordan look like a giant cat leaping through the air to catch his prey.

Ashley knew with a sinking feeling, exactly why both her parents were ordering her downstairs to talk.

"Ashley, NOW!" her mother yelled up impatiently.

Realizing that her borrowed time was up, Ashley slowly made her way downstairs to the living room where both her parents were sitting on the couch.

But, she thought, slightly confused, neither one looked mad. They looked - scared?

Ashley curled up in the uncomfortable, straight-backed chair across from them. She collected her legs into her chest and rested her chin on her bony kneecaps.

Her parents looked at each other using parental sign language - badly - in an attempt to agree on who would speak first. After a few rounds of this, it was decided it would be her father.

"Ash," he began, clasping his fingers together in a super tense teepee. "You know Cody wasn't in school today..."

Caught off guard by the non-volleyball related topic, she simply nodded and then laughed, rolling her eyes, "Yeah - faker."

Neither of her parents cracked a smile.

What. The. Heck.

"Honey, Cody's in the hospital," her mother nearly spit out the words she was so eager to get them out of her mouth.

"What? Why? Is he hurt?" Ashley asked, confused.

"No... Ash... " her dad said, "Cody has leukemia. He's had it for some time now but it got worse recently and finally last night Mr. and Mrs. Martin had to take him to the hospital," he continued.

Ashley hugged her knees even tighter to her body, absorbing the words. She saw that her mom was saying more things, but her parents had faded into a bubble, their images growing fuzzier with each word. Then, the bubble containing them lifted right up off the couch, floated in front of her, and went right out the living room window.

"Ash? Honey? Are you listening to us?" her mother's concerned voice sounded muffled and miles away.

Ashley began rocking gently back and forth in the chair, trying to form a coherent thought. All she could picture was Cody fast asleep at the planetarium in the dingy orange recliner chair. She hoped he was sleeping as peacefully in the hospital as he had that day. She remembered how difficult it had been to wake him up and how jealous she'd been that anyone could sleep that deeply in public. As she began wondering what the hospital ceiling looked like, her dad cut into her thoughts.

"Ash?" he prodded, sounding genuinely worried.

The bubble containing her parents had made its way back through the living room window, depositing them onto the couch. They were both looking at their daughter with wide eyes, as if she was a bomb that might suddenly explode.

Feeling the same way she had in gym class, wanting to disappear and hoping the floor would swallow her whole, Ashley jumped to her feet. She was better in motion anyway. She started pacing around the living room, wishing she had a basketball to occupy her hands.

"Yeah… so… what…" her racing brain searched for something to hold onto. "Is he - like - what - when is he coming home?" she asked.

Her parents exchanged a panicked look.

"Ash," her father said as her mother covered her face, clearly trying to keep Ashley from seeing her tears, "He's not."

Without a second thought, Ashley immediately stopped pacing and held her dad's gaze for several moments. Then, without a word, she simply walked out of the room, back upstairs to her bedroom, and quietly closed the door behind her.

She heard her mother break into sobs downstairs and quickly grabbed her phone to play music and drown it out. She retreated into her own bubble, crawling under the covers with her phone. Then she did the only thing she'd ever done when she was freaking out - she texted her best friend.

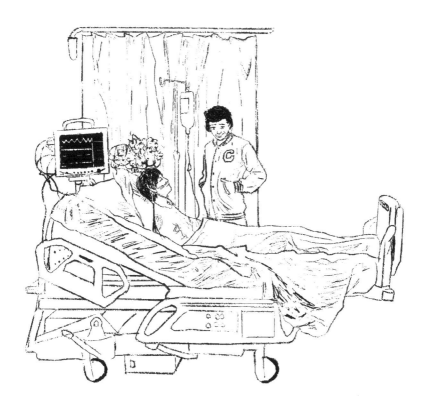

4
Blast Off

"Do you know who's in there with him?" Ashley asked the nurse who was standing outside Cody's glass cube in the pediatric ICU.

When she looked in she'd seen a tall figure through the curtain at Cody's bedside but couldn't make out who it was. Ashley decided to memorize every detail about the nurse, mainly as a way to avoid entering the cube. First, she looked too young to be a nurse and in charge of people's lives. She was standing at a medication cart preparing a tray of clear tiny plastic cups containing various colors of thick liquids that smelled sickeningly sweet, like super strong cotton candy - medicine made especially for kids. The young nurse was wearing happy animal print scrubs and had a stuffed koala bear clinging to the stethoscope around her neck. If it wasn't for the stack of syringes in sealed packages also on the tray, the nurse might have been preparing snacks for a kid's birthday party.

"His brother is in there with him. You can go in if you want, but just for five minutes - Cody gets tired easily," the nurse said with a reassuring smile before heading in the opposite direction with her tray.

Ashley stood outside the ajar glass sliding door, eavesdropping. She heard Cody's brother laugh.

"That's not exactly what college life is like, bro," he said.

The last time she'd seen Rick was at the going away cookout Cody's family had thrown for him before he left for UCLA a couple years ago.

Ashley finally stopped stalling and inhaled deeply, instantly wrinkling her nose at the smell of rubber gloves combined with rubbing alcohol mixed with the cotton candy smell of medicine. She fought the overwhelming urge to flee the scene, reminding herself sternly that this wasn't a stupid argument in gym class. This was real life.

And, she thought, *Cody needs me.*

As he would undoubtedly tell her if he was out in the hallway watching her right now, *"Suck it up, Ash!"*

So, she did. She slid the glass door open the rest of the way and entered Cody's glass cube. Rick pulled the curtain back and smiled when he saw her.

"Hey Ashley, good to see you again!"

She focused purposefully on Rick's eyes as she shook his hand.

"Hi, Rick…" was all she could think of to say.

"Well, I was just taking off to get some lunch, so I'll leave you guys alone," Rick said. "See you in a bit, little bro. Don't cause any trouble you two," he said with a forced smile.

Ashley saw out the corner of her eye Rick leaning down to hug Cody. She kept her eyes averted until the last moment, then finally slid her gaze over to the large, high-tech looking hospital bed that was surrounded by a ton of machines. Cody, hooked up to a zillion IV lines and cords coming from the machines, looked like a tiny black-haired hamster that got tangled up in a mess of giant vines in the middle of a jungle.

He smiled up at her weakly and lifted his hand in the shape of a fist. Ashley smiled and gently fist bumped him.

What the heck am I supposed to do with only five minutes? What should I say?

As usual, her best friend had her back.

"How're the Drama Girls?" he asked in an eerily quiet voice.

Trying not to obsess about how skinny and white he looked, Ashley thought back to the volleyball incident and tried to remember how angry and humiliated she'd felt in that moment. It was hard to feel any of those things now though. That stuff felt silly and from a different life. All she felt now was scared.

"They're fine… whatever," Ashley lied. "How are you?"

"Mainly bored," Cody said with an eyeroll, but then quickly added something that made Ashley's next breath catch in her throat - "I'm sick of waiting."

"Waiting for what?" she blurted out.

"I dunno," he shrugged, looking out the window.

Ashley thought of the bubble her parents were in and how it floated out the living room window. She wondered if her mind would make one for Cody too, then silently scolded herself for thinking it.

"Are you scared?" She snapped her jaw shut, surprised at her own question. She'd meant to ask how he felt but somehow those words got mixed up on the way out of her mouth.

What is WRONG with me???

But she didn't apologize because she realized she wanted to know the answer.

"No," Cody said, with surprising volume, "I'm just really tired. Like I need a really long nap."

"Well, in that case, we should go back to the planetarium because *nothing* could wake you up there." Ashley teased.

Cody was quiet for a minute, then said thoughtfully, "That's exactly what I'm hoping it will be - especially with the comfy chair and outer space all around."

"Coh!" Ashley gasped in horror.

"Ash, it's okay. They think I don't know but I do. And I'm okay with it," he said, sounding more adult than ever, Ashley thought, which was saying a lot since he'd always been like a little adult.

"How can you be okay with... not being here anymore?" Ashley said.

She also realized she was starting to feel anger bubbling up that Cody seemed unwilling to fight. If this were a basketball game, the person losing was expected to fight. Once again, she got mad at herself, creating a tug of war in her brain between feeling scared, angry, and guilty. Cody seemed to sense her dilemma.

"Ash it's not like I'm giving up. There's just nothing else anyone can do. What am I supposed to do, sit here and freak out?" he said.

"I don't know… I'd be angry and wanna fight though…" she blurted out and then slapped her hand over her face.

This time she did apologize, "Omigod, Coh, I'm so sorry!"

He let out a quiet chuckle, "Ash, the only thing you'd be able to fight in this situation would be the nurses and doctors trying to help you, and I can totally see you doing that because you're ridiculous sometimes."

She laughed in relief.

"Besides," he said, sounding tired again, "I've already fought. That's why I haven't had the energy to fight with *you* lately."

Ashley saw a little bit of a twinkle in his eyes when he said that last part. But by the time she blinked away some unexpected tears and looked back, the twinkle had faded. She could tell Cody was getting more tired and knew the nurse with the koala stethoscope would be back in soon to make her leave.

Her brain spun into overdrive trying to figure out what else to say. There were a million things. Ashley bit her lip and dug her fingernails into her palms to keep from melting down and blowing it.

"Coh… I…" she started awkwardly, "I hope you have a good nap."

Cody smiled and put his hand over hers. Now Ashley really had trouble not crying. She took a few deep breaths like she would do after missing a few key shots at the basket in a row, trying to get her head right again.

"Okay," she said, shaking away the tears that threatened to come out. "So when I come back tomorrow, we're going to watch the '98 finals against the Jazz, which was of course the *best* MJ moment of all time," she said. Ashley was fully expecting a debate because Cody thought the '89 playoffs were better, but Cody just lay there smiling at her and staring at her face, like he was memorizing it.

Then, suddenly, something caught Cody's attention behind her in the corner of the room. His dark thin eyebrows lifted at a tilt with curiosity. His eyes seemed to be tracking someone or something. Ashley turned but saw only an empty chair.

"Coh, are you okay?" she asked.

"Yeah," he said quietly. "I'm good. I'll be good - not alone."

Before Ashley could ask him what he meant by that, the nurse entered the glass cube carrying a humongous flower arrangement.

"For your collection," she said to Cody with a laugh.

Ashley hadn't noticed until that moment that the room was nearly packed with flower arrangements, many with balloons, and cheerful greeting cards everywhere. Suddenly noticing the array of colors made her dizzy. She wondered why she was only just noticing them now.

"Okay, that's it, young lady. Time to go," the nurse said with a sweet smile after she put the flowers down.

Ashley fist bumped her best friend one last time.

"Okay bud, I'll see you tomorrow. We're watching the game," she said almost too forcefully.

Cody simply nodded and closed his eyes with a peaceful smile on his face.

"Nite, nite," she whispered as she left the room, purposefully not looking back.

Outside the cube she ran into Rick, as well as Cody's mom and dad. They looked like wilted plants.

"Thanks for coming here honey, I know that means a lot to Cody," his mom said, rubbing Ashley's shoulder.

Ashley had the urge to give her a big reassuring hug but she thought the poor woman might break if she touched her too hard. Then, she and Cody's dad turned around and walked slowly back into the cube.

"C'mon," said Rick, "I'll walk you to the elevator."

Ashley nodded and they started walking.

"This might sound weird, but did my brother ever look into the corner of the room at nothing?" Rick asked.

"Yeah," Ashley said, surprised, "What was that about?"

Rick shrugged as they reached the bank of elevators at the end of the ICU.

"I don't know exactly," he pondered, pressing the down arrow for her. "I crashed in there on a foldaway bed so our parents could go home last night. I woke up in the middle of the night and Cody was having a whole conversation with someone in the corner named Gabe."

"Huh," Ashley said, trying to remember if she'd ever seen Cody talking to himself before. She wondered if it was the cotton candy medicine doing weird things to his head.

"Yeah, but then this morning he said he had no idea what I was talking about," Rick said.

They both avoided eye contact by watching the floor numbers light up as the elevator approached the ICU.

"Do you guys know anyone named Gabe?" he asked.

Ashley wracked her brain, thinking.

"Nope," she said as the elevator arrived. "Not at school anyway."

"Hmmm," Rick said, looking down at the floor and frowning.

Before getting in the elevator, Ashley awkwardly punched Rick lightly on the shoulder.

"Hang in there, dude," she said, feeling like a total dork.

Rick nodded, pursing his lips together and looking away thoughtfully into space as the elevator doors slid shut in front of her. He looked exactly like Cody in that moment.

Alone in the elevator, Ashley dropped down onto the floor in a squat and bawled her eyes out. She looked up and saw her small reflection in the mirrored elevator ceiling. She felt like the last person on earth. In a weird way - she was jealous of Cody's upcoming trip into outer space.

5
The Bell Hangers

The four Great Halls led directly into the center ring of a wagon wheel design. The hallways were lined with videos embedded into the golden gilded walls. The video galleries showed lively, vivid scenes of people enjoying various aspects of life on earth - babies being born, birthday parties, falling in love, getting married, enjoying nature, traveling to beautiful parts of the world, sports, music, art, and other moments of sheer joy and happiness.

The four Great Halls came together in the Bell Room. It was the only room in this place that didn't have an infinitely high ceiling, blindingly bright lights all around, and a layer of clouds hovering around your knees. The Bell Room was a perfectly "ordinary" room, other than the fact that it seemed to stretch on forever. The room was full of white folding chairs littered about, as if a meeting were about to take place but nobody had bothered to put the chairs into proper rows yet. This was intentional. These chairs were meant to stand on, not sit on. All around the room were stacks of party decorations - giant colorful rolls of streamers, balloons, paper plates, party games, and everything else that would make for the best birthday party ever. It was a place where people gathered, explored, sat on benches and reflected, listened to beautiful music, or simply walked amongst the knee high clouds and enjoyed being there. It was a place with no stress, only happiness and love.

This was heaven.

Gabe the Bell Keeper was walking quickly down the east Great Hall carrying his trusty clipboard as usual. There was a lot of work to do today. He arrived at the Bell Room and opened the ordinary looking door, looking around at the bustle of activity in the room. There were many bells to be hung today. Nearly every chair was occupied. People of all ages and races, wearing a variety of different clothing from all cultures and time periods of history, stood on the chairs. They were all hanging beautiful golden bells from hooks in the ceiling. Each bell seemed to emerge from a glimmering gold spiral and had on it a heart made from angel wings.

In addition to those standing on chairs hanging bells, there were a ton of other people throughout the room sifting through huge piles of party decorations, picking out things they liked.

Gabe moved among his bell hangers, checking names off his clipboard, and smiling at each person in turn.

"Exciting day isn't it?" he said to a middle-aged, dark-skinned woman hanging a bell with the name "Ruewenna" engraved on it.

"My daughter," the woman explained to Gabe. "Of course she's a lot older than me now!"

"Yes, and that's such a unique name," Gabe replied with admiration.

"It means a beautiful, intelligent, confident woman with high standards who doesn't back down from a challenge," the woman said, bursting with pride. "Well, at least we know where she got that last part from," she indicated with a nod over to an elderly couple who were playing an obviously competitive game of chess at a small folding table in the corner.

"You sure you want to play that move again?" the man said to the woman with a mischievous smile. "You've played it a million times and it hasn't worked yet!"

"Oh hush and focus on your own game, Harold!" the woman retorted peering intently at the chess board over her bifocals.

"Ruewenna's even more headstrong than her grandparents, Gabe," the woman on the chair hanging her bell said, "You'll see soon enough!" she added with a wink.

"I can't wait to meet her," Gabe said, unable to wipe the smile off his face from the excitement of the day.

He moved on with his clipboard to check on the other bell hangers. It was never boring in the Bell Room, but today it seemed even more of a party than usual. Gabe reached a particularly rowdy group in the center of the room. They were a mix of all ages and genders and a blend of cultures including Indian, Asian, and Native American.

Most of the people in the group had some variation of black hair. They were causing quite a commotion with their raucous laughter and good natured teasing of one another.

"Hey now, am I going to have to send you all to separate halls?" Gabe teased, joining the outer ring of the group.

"Sorry Gabe," the elderly woman in Native American garb in the center of the group said with a laugh.

As the designated bell hanger, she was obviously the elder stateswoman of the group.

"But we're just SO excited to see him!" she said.

Just then, an already hung bell in another part of the room began to ring loudly. It was the most beautiful sound ever made - one that could not exist on earth because it was too perfect for earthly ears to hear. A man dashed into the room seemingly from thin air and stood under his bell, his head tilted upward, eyes closed and smiling as if enjoying a warm sunny day. The name "Jacob" was engraved on the bell. Only Gabe seemed to notice the man, as Cody's family members were busy with their party preparations.

The man opened his eyes and turned to Gabe to explain. "My wife was just remembering the time we overturned our canoe while taking wedding photos. The two of us AND the photographer all ended up in the lake with soaking wet wedding clothes. Thankfully the wedding was already over and she had a good sense of humor about it," Jacob said with a laugh.

"That's a great memory," Gabe remarked to Jacob.

Gabe looked around the room at other bells that were occasionally ringing. When they did, the people whose names were on the bells rushed to stand under their own bells, basking in the special moments of being remembered by those still on earth.

Jacob stood under his bell for a moment longer, enjoying the sound of its ring. Then, he blew a kiss at it as it became still again, and left the Bell Room, going about his day.

A middle-aged woman, a newcomer to heaven who had been watching Jacob curiously, waited until he left before approaching Gabe.

"Excuse me, what was that man just doing?" she asked and pointed at Jacob's bell, which was now hanging silently on its hook.

"Ah, well," Gabe said, his face lighting up, always excited to explain how the bells work. "Each person here has a Heaven's Bell hung somewhere in this room. Your bell is hung by loved ones, who are already in heaven, right before you arrive here. When your bell rings, it means that someone down on earth is thinking of you, cherishing the time they got to spend with you. It's a reminder of how much you're loved and that even though you are now here in heaven, you are not forgotten."

"That's so nice," the woman said as her face lit up with happiness. "So Jacob heard his bell ringing and came to the bell room to find out who was thinking of him?"

"That's right, and also to share in the love and memories with them, no matter how long they've been here. In Jacob's case, he has been here for about one earth year, but his wife who is still down there, was dusting photographs in the living room and was suddenly reminded of their wedding photos of a soaking wet bride and groom. As she remembered that day, Jacob's bell up here began to ring," Gabe chuckled at the image in his mind of Jacob and his wife in their formal wedding clothes, falling out of their canoe but laughing the whole time.

"That is funny," the woman agreed. "Thank you for explaining that Gabe."

Meanwhile, the rowdy group in the center of the room had resumed their party preparations as the elderly woman in the center finished hanging the bell and stepped down from the chair onto the floor.

"Now," she said with authority, "let's go check on the final touches to my great-great-great grandson's basketball court."

The group enthusiastically finished gathering up their party decorations and poured out of the Bell Room.

Gabe looked up at the name on the bell: "Cody Martin."

He checked Cody's name off on his clipboard and continued with his rounds.

6
Goodbye For Here

"Dad, I have to tell you something," Ashley said, gnawing away on her bottom lip, which was losing actual layers of skin from how much she'd been chewing on it lately.

She was sitting on a barstool in the kitchen, scrolling mindlessly on her phone to keep her mind off of Cody. Her dad was over at the sink washing dishes.

"Tell me," he said, half turning around with a grin, elbows deep in suds.

"C'mon, it's serious," she said and he could tell by her face that it was.

He turned the water off and joined his daughter at the counter, drying his hands on a dish towel.

"Is it about Cody, kiddo?"

"No," she said with a sad sigh thinking about her almost-gone friend. "It's actually about mom."

Her dad tilted his head in an emotional question mark. Ashley hurried forward with her thought before she lost the nerve.

"I know about the baby... I mean from last year... I know mom was pregnant... but then... not."

Her father stared at her in shock but then shook his head with a kind of smirk. "I've always known you were sharper and smarter than anyone else your age Ash, and this is proof," he said, "How did you know?"

"Well, before you give me any more genius points, I should tell you that it wasn't that hard. I overheard you guys talking about it," she said. "I think you both think I spend more time in my room than I really do."

"Well, you basically only exist there, on basketball courts, at school, and at Cody's," her father laughed but then cut himself short at the last words.

Ashley hung her head and tried to hide behind her hair, which she was uncharacteristically wearing down around her face.

"Sorry," he said, patting her hand with still damp hands.

Ashley stayed quiet for a minute, composing herself.

"Do you guys know what the sex was?" she finally asked.

"Uh... yeah," her dad hesitated. "It was a boy."

Ashley grabbed onto the sides of the barstool to steady herself from the wave of emotion that washed over her.

I almost had a brother - for real.

Then her mind went back to the current closest thing she had to a brother, laying in his hospital bed, bravely preparing for his trip into outer space.

"Dad, do you think the baby went to the same place as Cody's going?"

Her father breathed out hard, making a sputtering sound with his mouth and planting his chin on his cupped hands thoughtfully.

"I don't know, kiddo, but my best guess would be yes. That's what you learned in bible class for all those years, right?"

"Yeah," she said.

But all those years of sitting in the church basement listening to stories and theories about people who were long dead, suddenly seemed like wispy smoke images that would dissolve into thin air if you blew on them too hard. What happened to her almost baby brother and now to Cody, was real.

"I just want to make sure he's going to be okay - not alone or anything," she said.

Ashley pulled more of her hair around her face, determined not to fall apart in front of the man she respected more than anyone in the world. To her dad's credit, he pretended not to notice, gazing out the kitchen window in deep thought, continuing to pat her hand absentmindedly.

"I know," he said. "You've been a good friend to him though. And I'm sure he knows that."

That was more than Ashley could take. She nodded then climbed off the barstool so quickly that she nearly fell down. Without another word, she ran out of the kitchen toward her room. But when she made it to the top of the stairs, her phone rang - a video call from Cody.

Ashley sprinted the rest of the way down the hall to her bedroom, slamming the door shut behind her. She sat at her desk and answered the call immediately, flicking her desk lamp on so Cody would be able to see her.

"Coh," she said.

She anxiously held the phone close, peering wide-eyed into the screen. Cody had an oxygen mask strapped to his face that seemed bigger than his whole head. She could tell by how hard his chest and shoulders were heaving up and down that even with the oxygen, it was still hard for him to breathe. Ashley wished she could breathe for him - she had tons of extra air right now that she didn't know what to do with. She gripped her phone tightly, staring at Cody.

It finally hit her - *he's dying.*

Her own breathing sped up and she dug her finger-nails into her palm to try and slow it down. The weird part was that Cody didn't look scared at all. He had that same freaky calm look in his eyes that she'd seen off and on for months now.

Suddenly his phone flipped around and she found her-self face to face with Rick, who waved at Ashley with a solemn smile. She spotted two other shadows in the corner and knew they were Cody's mom and dad.

On one hand, she felt like an intruder but on the other and more important hand, she only wanted to talk to Cody and didn't care what it took. The phone flipped back around so it was facing Cody again.

"Coh - does it hurt?" she blurted out, not caring how she sounded.

It's not about me.

Cody nodded but he didn't have enough air to get words out. It was obvious he had something to tell her though. Rick leaned in so Cody could whisper in his ear.

Turning to the camera, his voice choked up, Rick said to the screen, "He just said - sister."

That's all he could get out before turning away from the phone and his little brother.

"I love you too, Coh," Ashley said, now in a full-on ugly cry.

Cody nodded and she thought she saw a smile behind the giant oxygen mask.

Then, the call suddenly ended. Ashley gasped in surprise that her goodbye was over that quickly. She wanted to tell him so many things - that her brother would keep him company, to send her signs about what it was like up there, that she loved him like a brother... there were so many words that she still had inside. Wiping her tears off the phone screen, she settled for one thing to say, and prayed to God that Cody could hear her, wherever he was.

"Goodbye for here," Ashley whispered, kissing the blank screen.

7
Outer Space

The last thing Cody remembered was seeing Ash sobbing on his phone screen as Rick held the device up in front of his face. He remembered, almost as a distant memory, feeling horrible for making her cry. He was going to miss Ashley so much. Then, the world went dark. He felt as if he'd suddenly fallen asleep. When Cody opened his eyes, he was somewhere new. It was so bright that at first, he had to shield his eyes. Once they finally adjusted, he squinted and looked up, expecting to see the source of the bright lights. But instead, he was shocked by what he saw above him.

It was outer space!

It wasn't the fake glow-in-the-dark planets and stars that his parents stuck all over his bedroom ceiling when he was little either. This was *real* outer space - he could feel the cool air and bigness all around him. Cody's next thought was whether he and Ashley got it right, that heaven was outer space, or if God made it outer space just for him. Then he realized he didn't care.

This is awesome!

Then Cody made another incredible discovery - for the first time in what felt like forever, there was no pain and he had no trouble breathing. He still couldn't believe how quickly he'd gone from being able to play basketball with Ashley one day, to not even having enough energy to hold a basketball the next. Even though his parents and the doctors had explained what was happening because of his quickly worsening illness, Cody had felt like he had been torn from a perfectly good, healthy body and put in a broken shell. Even talking had been a struggle.

He tried sitting up in the bed, since that was one of the things he hadn't been able to do on earth for a couple weeks before dying, and he popped right up in the bed with the littlest effort - no problem at all! He smiled triumphantly and raised his arms over his head in victory.

If sitting was that easy, maybe…

"And the crowd goes wild, agggghhhhhhh!" he shouted. He was surprised by how strong his voice sounded. He half expected it to echo, since he was in outer space and all. But it didn't; it sounded like he was in his own bedroom. Then, Cody realized he wasn't alone. He turned around in the bed and saw a crowd of people standing in the corner of a bright bedroom watching him.

At the front of the crowd was a beautiful, tan skinned older woman wearing an animal skin dress decorated with bright colors of paint and beads. Her arms and neck were covered with large, elaborate necklaces and bracelets. Cody guessed, based on his social studies class, that she was from the Cheyenne tribe of Native Americans. He gawked in awe at her long beautiful salt and pepper hair that appeared to be made of silk, braided to the side and held with a beaded clip.

"Welcome my great-great-great grandson!" the woman said softly, holding her arms open.

At first, remembering worries from earth about talking to strangers, Cody hesitated. But then, sensing the specialness and safety of his new home (although, he still wasn't ready to say its name out loud), he ran into the woman's loving arms and hugged her tightly. A single word came into his mind...

"Welcome home, dear," she said, kissing him on top of his head.

Home.

That was exactly how Cody felt. But he still had loads of questions popping up in his head.

He pulled away and looked up at the woman. "Is that what I call you? Great-great-great grandma? That's a long title."

She laughed, "Grandmother will be just fine. We're all your grandmothers and grandfathers up here. There will not be any confusion."

Cody nodded and scanned the crowd of people behind her, noting how many of them had dark black hair like him. He was used to his hair color standing out from other people's more "normal" blonde or brown hair.

He was also in awe of how many family members he suddenly had. He didn't get to see his grandparents on earth all that much; his parents always said they lived too far away and everyone was always too busy to see each other, anyways. Cody was excited to meet all his new grandparents here, where nobody was ever too busy, but he frowned at his next question.

"What about my best friend, Ashley? Will she be okay?" His new grandmother knelt down eye level with him.

"Yes, she will. However..." she looked at the other members of Cody's family in attendance and they nodded at her in silent agreement. "...we were going to start with your basketball court."

Cody's face perked up with interest.

His grandmother gave a little chuckle and continued on. "But there will be plenty of time for that. There's something special I want to show you first."

She took his hand and led him out of the bright little bedroom. They walked, more like waded, through wispy, light, knee-deep clouds that appeared to cover an endless white field. Cody could make out vague shapes of people moving around but he wasn't clear on exactly what he was seeing. He gripped his grandmother's hand and kept walking, still in awe of how *good* his body felt, how *peaceful* he felt all the way through. He'd never felt anything like this in his entire life!

It seemed like within moments they were approaching the largest most beautiful golden doors he'd ever seen. Cody was overwhelmed with a feeling of warmth that started in his toes and worked its way up to the top of his head.

His jaw dropped in awe as the gigantic gold doors swayed noiselessly inward, opening into an immense hallway with video screens built into the walls. The hallway was extremely fancy, like what the largest and best royal castle in the world must look like. Without being told, Cody knew from inside his mind that this was called "the Great Hall." He and his grandmother walked together down the hall, hand in hand, family reunited.

Something caught Cody's eye on one of the screens. He gasped, dropped his grandmother's hand, and ran across what he now noticed was the shiniest, slickest, white marble floor ever - like an ice rink. He nearly slipped but caught himself on the wall as he arrived at the video screen and pressed his face into it to get a closer look.

It looked like a home movie of he and Ashley at a Bulls game together last spring. The video seemed to be shot by someone standing right in front of them. As their parents occasionally talked amongst themselves (but mostly checked their phones and drank beer), Cody and Ashley were totally engrossed with each other. They shared a large messy paper tray of nachos that covered both their hands in layers of cheese, salsa, and sour cream. They were more occupied with trying to make the other one laugh harder by making wisecracks about the other team's players, people in the stands - whatever material they could find to send the other person into hysterics.

Cody stared at the screen longingly, waiting for feelings of sadness to set in.

But the sadness didn't come. Instead, all he felt was a continuous wave of pure love and joy washing over him. He was grateful for every moment he got to spend on earth with Ashley. In addition to the moments flashing by on the video screen, he remembered all the other moments too - all at the same time. It was the best feeling ever!

Then, he heard a bell ringing. First it sounded far away but then gradually it got closer. It was the most musical, incredible sound he'd ever heard- yet another mind blowing moment in his day of firsts.

Was it still the same day?

He turned away from the video screen and looked up at his grandmother inquiringly.

She smiled, "She must be thinking of you, too." But she could tell by her grandson's face that he didn't understand. "Come Cody, let's go visit your bell," she said, as if that made perfect sense.

When they arrived in the Bell Room in all its glory- when he saw all the perfect bells hanging from the ceiling and all the happy people standing underneath them- he understood. He looked up at his bell, and in that one object, finally understood the perfection of heaven in a way that nobody on earth ever would.

The bell is pure love.

"This is your very own Heaven's Bell, Cody," his grandmother explained as he unfolded a chair and scrambled onto it to get a closer look at his brand new shiny bell. It was even more perfect up close. Cody could not resist. He had to find out what it felt like. He reached his hand out but his grandmother quickly stopped him.

"No, Cody. Please don't touch that," she said, but still with a smile.

"I figured there wouldn't be rules here," Cody said with a good-natured laugh.

"That's mostly true, my love, but there's a good reason for this rule."

"What's that?" he asked.

"You never know when it might start -"

The words were barely out of his grandmother's mouth when Cody was startled - a lot - as in, almost falling off the chair startled - when his bell started ringing - *loudly*! He instinctively covered his ears with his hands but then realized the sound did not hurt them. He looked down at his grandmother for an explanation.

"Someone down there is thinking of you."

Cody had no doubt as to whom.

Down another one of the Great Halls, even though he wasn't watching it, a video screen showed Ashley in her driveway basketball court, shooting hoops by herself, obviously deep in thought. Then, a thin, strikingly pretty African American girl entered from the side of the screen and walked up the driveway toward her.

8
No Drama

Ashley first met Bianca, a quiet but friendly girl, on a Saturday morning. It was about a week after Cody's funeral, and Ashley was biking past the huge baby blue house that she'd always dreamed of living in at the end of the cul-de-sac, when she noticed boxes and furniture scattered all over the front yard. A man and woman, about her parents' ages, grunted as they carried object after object into the house. Meanwhile, a petite but athletic looking girl, presumably their daughter, was walking on her hands around the lawn, steering her body nimbly through the mess.

Ashley stopped her bike on the sidewalk and watched for a few moments before calling out to the girl.

"Where'd you learn how to do that?" Ashley shouted.

Bianca flipped her tiny feet over her head and back onto the soft, dewy grass. She looked over at Ashley and gave a small smile and shrug. "You know... after school gymnastics."

Ashley got off her bike, kicked the stand down and found a box to sit on.

"Not really. I play basketball. I didn't know we had gymnastics."

"Well, you do," Bianca informed her, somewhat author-itatively, sliding easily into splits on the grass to make her point.

Ashley's eyebrows went up in an amused, curious way. *Who is this girl?*

"There's a gym near the train station," Bianca said. "It's very good. They have trophies and everything."

Ashley nodded, studying Bianca like a science project.

"Yeah, cool, but do you play *regular* sports too?" she asked Bianca.

Now it was Bianca's eyebrows that rose.

Ashley's question triggered a brief but friendly argument wherein the new girl "educated" Ashley about how dance and gymnastics *were* real sports. Ashley took her word for it and after that, the girls became fast friends, which wasn't surprising. From the moment she saw that freaky girl walk-ing around the lawn on her hands, Ashley knew that Bianca would not fit in with the *dram-ah* girls. The Drama Girls were fiercely committed to "acting normal" and basically being clones of one another. Playing circus on your front lawn in front of the whole neighborhood would not do. Bianca would need a good, loyal, fellow freak to keep her company.

Ashley somehow talked Bianca into letting her teach her how to play basketball in exchange for handstand lessons. Ashley's parents were highly amused at the idea of their otherwise serious, highly competitive daughter casually walking around on her hands. But overall, they were thrilled to see her make a new friend.

"Okay," Ashley told Bianca, relishing her new role as "coach" while lining up for a two-point bucket. "First, you wanna plant your feet like this… you know, those things that *you* usually have in the air," she wise-cracked.

"Ha, Ha, HA," Bianca cracked back good naturedly from across the driveway.

Ashley smiled, happy to have a new sparring partner, even though her heart was still hurting at the loss of her last and most special one.

The lesson went really well, Bianca picked up basketball surprisingly fast. More importantly, Ashley and Bianca got along really well! But there was one moment in particular that made Ashley almost feel back to normal again…

***

By now, Cody had made his way back to the monitors. His Heaven's Bell had been nearly ringing right off its hook and he was eager to find out why. He watched on the monitor as Ashley attempted to fake out the new girl on the driveway court. Ashley started to raise her arms to shoot the ball, only to lower them and continue dribbling toward the basket.

"Wow, still making those obvious fouls, ey Ash?" Cody laughed at the screen.

But rather than call her on it, the new girl swooped in, stole the ball from Ashley and made a perfect 3-pointer!

Instead of getting angry, Ashley walked quietly over to the decorative bench and sat down for a minute, covering her face with her hair, pretending to catch her breath. Cody could tell what she was really doing though. That girl had unknowingly, almost perfectly replicated what he would have done in that situation.

He placed his hand on the screen. "It's okay Ash, I may be here in outer space, but I'll always be there with you too," he said, mentally willing her to hear his words, or at least feel them.

From inside the Bell Room, he could hear his bell reaching fever pitch.

"Okay already, I hear you! Now, stop thinking about me and get your head back in the game, girl!" Cody laughed. Then he turned and walked back down the hall, disappearing into a bright hazy light at the other end. He was eager to go strike up a game on his *own* basketball court.

On the video screen Ashley raised her head, pushed her hair from her face, and smiled at Bianca. Then, with a playful grin, she snatched the ball from her new friend and drove toward the basket once again.

9
The Message

"Ashley, for the last time - BREAKFAST!!!"

Sitting in bed, writing in a journal propped up against her tented knees, Ashley looked up briefly at her bedroom door toward the sound of her mom's screech. She thought for a second before quickly returning to scribbling furiously in her Bulls branded notebook. Her focus was less on her rumbling stomach and more on her racing mind. That dream was *way* too real.

"Ash, you up?" her dad called from the hall.

"Yeah, come on in."

He cracked the door open and poked his head through, "Morning glory, exactly how much trouble are you trying to get yourself into?"

She didn't seem to hear him, still scribbling as if her life depended on it. He stood there quietly watching until she finally spoke.

"Dad, have you ever had a dream *so* real that you couldn't shake it off even, like..." she looked at her smart watch, "...an hour later?"

Her father opened her bedroom door all the way, crossed his arms at the elbows and gazed upward as he contemplated.

"Sure, I guess. Not recently, but I had some pretty vivid dreams when I was your age. Why? What was your dream about?"

Ashley finally finished scribbling, closed her notebook and set it aside on the bed. She wrapped her arms around her legs and rested her chin on her knees.

"Guess?" she said.

"Ah," her father said knowingly.

She nodded and the two sat in silence for a moment. Ashley was thinking about the past year- about learning to live without the person who'd practically been attached to her hip since kindergarten.

The silence was soon broken by her quite irritated mom, who had come out of the kitchen and was calling up the stairs. "Okay missy, I left your breakfast on the stove. I have to go to work."

"Thanks mom - sorry!" Ashley called back, shrugging at her dad apologetically.

"I'll make sure she eats, don't worry, honey. Love you!" he called out.

Ashley smiled gratefully at him- her eternal defender.

"So, about the dream," he prompted, taking a seat at her desk.

Ashley arranged her legs to sit criss cross and leaned forward eagerly.

"Usually, my Cody dreams are like normal dream stuff - random memories and also him showing up in my regular life now. Like, I'll be doing handstands with B and suddenly Cody starts dribbling a basketball in circles around us but doesn't look at us or say anything. He's like a hologram," she said. "You know - random."

"But this time?"

"This time - he was talking TO me dad! And it was just the two of us. We were sitting on the bench in the driveway, he was wearing that Jordan jersey he loved, with the rip by the neck, and he had his black high tops on with white socks…" Ashley rambled breathlessly, faster and faster.

"Whoa, there," her dad laughed and held his hands up in a "timeout" T. "Honey slow down - breathe."

Ashley took a deep breath and tried to get control of all the thoughts and images that were fluttering around in her mind like a swarm of butterflies hopped-up on Red Bull.

"See," she said and indicated the notebook on the bed next to her, "This is why I was trying to write it down. I can barely keep track of all the details and I don't want to lose anything. It's too important…. It was just SO good, you know - to see him again."

Her eyes briefly lost their focus as she stared over her dad's shoulder at the collage on the wall with photos of herself and Cody that she'd made shortly after his death.

"Does that make sense?" she asked, returning her gaze to her dad.

He smiled reassuringly. "Perfect sense honey."

"But I haven't even told you the best part," she said and her eyes sparkled with excitement. "It was what he TOLD me about while we were sitting on the bench. That's mainly what I wanted to remember after I woke up. That's the stuff I was writing down in my journal."

"Well, honey, I'm on the edge of my seat - tell me!" her dad said as he moved forward to the edge of her desk chair to make his point.

Ashley nodded, opened her Bulls notebook to make sure she didn't miss any details, settled back into her pillows, and told her dad everything Cody had told her about the "Heaven's Bells."

***

Many Years Later

Cody had long ago stopped trying to count how much earth time was passing down there. Mostly because of how *busy* he was up here. There was lots of basketball to be played on his own private court, not to mention all the regular reunion parties to be planned whenever new members of his family arrived. It didn't matter that he'd never met most of them in real life - everyone was long lost and eagerly embraced. It was as if they'd all known each other since the beginning of time.

There were also various other "angel projects" that he regularly signed up for with Gabe; ways to secretly provide guidance and direction to people on earth without their knowing about it. No two projects were ever the same and Cody always had a blast working alongside family members and new friends he'd met since arriving here.

His favorite part, however, was a place called "Moments"- something he'd discovered shortly after arriving. He remembered when he mistook the small square building for a movie theater.

When he'd first walked in, it did look like a movie theater but it was totally empty. He took a seat in the center of the room and waited to see if a movie would start but the room remained dark and the brightly lit white screen, blank.

What the heck?? He'd thought. Just as he was about to get up and leave, he remembered the time he and Ash had gone to the movies and this same thing had happened. They'd found out later that the projectionist had eaten some bad tuna salad for lunch and was stuck in the men's room barfing his brains out. Meanwhile, the audience waited impatiently for someone to press the computerized button to start the show.

Cody chuckled at the memory. He remembered how he and Ashley had started making up their own comical stories about why the movie wasn't starting, each scenario more hilarious than the last. By time the lights went down and the actual movie began playing, the two were in such hysterics that an usher rushed over and threatened to kick them out.

Suddenly, Cody realized he wasn't just reminiscing anymore - he was *living* the memory! Even though he knew it was impossible, there was Ashley in the movie seat next to him, her long bony legs curled up as usual, with tears streaming down her face from laughter. Cody almost fell out of his seat.

"Ash???" he said incredulously.

"Yeah? What, Coh? OMG that was hilarious, I'm DYING!" she said, wiping tears from her eyes grinning at him.

Cody turned and looked at the empty movie theater around him. So many questions were popping into his mind about what was happening. Then he remembered that here in heaven, sometimes as soon as you wondered about something, the answer would instantly pop into your head. He quickly posed the mental question - *What IS this place???*. The answer immediately popped into his mind - this was called a "Moments" theater, a place where you could relive, learn from, and treasure your favorite earth memories.

At first, as a lot of newbies did, Cody started hanging out in the various "Moments" theaters way too much. But then, his grandmother took him aside and gently reminded him that one of the greatest joys of heaven was creating *new* memories with family members he'd never met. After that, Cody had gradually lessened his time spent in the little theaters located all throughout heaven, the same as he'd done with the video screens in the Great Halls.

Walking by the Great Halls today, he found himself trying to recall the last time he'd specifically visited the video monitors to check on his loved ones still on earth.

It had been awhile.

Sure, he ran up and down the halls nearly every time his bell rang- he'd rush to the Bell Room and stand under the most beautiful, perfect sound in the world while he reminisced from afar with someone down there. But after a while, the video monitors along the way seemed to fade into the ornate walls and Cody eventually stopped pausing to look at the moving images on the screens.

Until today.

He wasn't sure what made him stop and look today, but yet another lesson he'd learned up here was to trust your instincts.

Once inside the brilliant golden hall, he pressed his face against the nearest video screen. It was as if the screen knew he was coming and flickered to life. It played a reel of short videos - all of Ashley. Many included closeup images of her speaking. He sensed that what she was saying was important so Cody felt around the monitor until he found the volume knob on the side and turned it up so he could watch AND listen to the scenes playing out on the screen.

The first scene showed Ashley at around the same age she was when Cody left her, telling her friend Bianca the story of Heaven's Bell as they practiced handstands and splits together on a lawn (Cody was shocked at first - *Ashley the gymnast??*). Then, in the next video, Ashley was at her computer writing a story for her school newspaper called - "Heaven's Bell."

Then it hit Cody... *she got my messages!!!*

He stepped back from the monitor and did a dorky little happy dance in the Great Hall, much to the amusement of a few of his friends passing by. One of them gave him the thumbs up sign - they knew how great it felt when a message sent to a loved one back on earth was received. It was the best feeling in this world! Cody returned to the monitor to see more.

In the next scene Ashley looked to be college age, now telling the story to a group of elderly people at a care facility where she was volunteering. Next, and now in her twenties, Ashley was a school teacher, leading a class of little kids in making heaven's bells as an arts and crafts project. Cody was personally impressed with the amount of glitter that was involved. "Right on, Ash," he whispered at the screen.

The video moved forward to the next scene. Ashley was now at home, a married woman with kids of her own. She was washing dishes at the kitchen sink and watching out the window as her young son and his friends played in the backyard. As they played, and as boys do, they shouted conversations back and forth. Ashley smiled with pride as she heard Michael telling his friends the same story she'd been telling him since he was a baby.

When the final scene came into focus on the video screen, Cody gasped as he realized that the elderly woman laying in her bed, covered in blankets with (of course) a vintage Bulls blanket on top - was Ashley. She appeared to be somewhere between asleep and awake as her family stood vigil, a now middle-aged Michael holding her hand.

Cody immediately turned down the volume knob and took off running down the Great Hall toward the Bell Room. As soon as he left it, the video screen went blank before resuming its normally scheduled programming. He made his way through the Bell Room, weaving through all the chairs, families, celebrations, boxes of party supplies, and, of course the endless sea of glowing, shiny bells hanging overhead. He finally reached a whole other room *beyond* the Bell Room. This one was also infinite but the ceiling was even lower and it was much quieter and darker, almost somber but peaceful, with only the occasional visitor. The bells here were each enclosed in their own glass box, all arranged in neat, symmetrical rows on endless glass counters – Cody had always thought of it as the world's largest jewelry store.

These were the bells of the living.

He tracked down Ashley's bell immediately, as if sensing her presence in a crowded room. He picked up the glass box and examined the bell inside. As he suspected after watching that last video scene, the bell inside was nearly rusted over, its ringer detached and lying on the floor of the box, having already fallen off.

Suddenly, Gabe was at Cody's side, carrying his trusty clipboard as usual. He smiled at Cody as he checked a box on his list.

"Ashley has obviously lived a full life. That's why her living bell is so worn. It looks like she'll need a brand new bell soon, one for this new chapter of her life," Gabe said with a smile.

"Yes," Cody said, feeling an enormous wave of warmth and pure love wash all over him, "I have just the one."

10
Reunion

Cody stepped down from the folding chair, tilted his head upward and admired his handiwork.

"It's your best one yet, bro," a voice behind him said.

"Thanks Rick," Cody said, turning to smile at his big brother.

He was still the same handsome college student Cody remembered, even though in reality, Rick had been a grandfather of five in his seventies when he died. Up here, you saw people the way you wanted to remember them.

"In fact," Rick teased, "I'm a little jealous because Ashley's bell here is *much* better than the plain ol' tin can you hung for me when I got here."

"Oh, you leave your little brother alone," their mother said, emerging from the larger than normal crowd attending the bell hanging, a mix of Cody's and Ashley's intergenerational families.

"It HAS to be the best one," Cody said with a ginormous smile on his still eleven year old face, "my best friend is on her way!"

***

Ashley was dreaming of clouds - endless rows of fluffy white clouds in a perfect blue sky. She thought maybe she was on an airplane. But, she wondered, feeling slightly disconnected from her body - *when did I get on an airplane?* The last thing she remembered was being at home in her bed under all her blankets with Michael, his daughter Amanda, and various other friends and family surrounding her. Even as she lay there, she could feel herself sliding out of her body away from them - quite the experience.

So THIS is what it's like!

She'd been wondering, literally for years, as she watched people die, starting with Cody all those years ago when they were kids.

Ashley kept floating through the clouds, feeling very relaxed but also with a distant feeling of her mind racing (as usual). But for some reason, unlike in normal times, it didn't bother her. Everything felt.... okay. So she kept floating until suddenly she was lying in bed and looking up at - the planetarium ceiling?

What the heck?

Ashley wanted a closer look, so she craned her neck and began working on the usual effort it took to lift her hand. She wanted to beckon someone to come help her up so she could get a better look at the ceiling- fully expecting to spot the cracks and water stains behind the stars and planets. But to her surprise, with the smallest effort, her arm flew lightly into the air, like an uprooted feather. She looked at it. It looked like her regular old arm - dry, wrinkled, with blue veins showing through the skin.

Well, what do you want? I'm freakin' 90 years old!

She continued to test her body until finally she was swinging her wrinkly old legs around and dangling them off the side of the bed with ease.

Okay, now what?

"It's about time loser!"

A familiar voice in the corner of the room startled her. She looked over and...

WHOA, flash from the past!

Ashley laughed, a gravelly but hearty laugh from dry, old vocal chords. Then she stood, a hunched over, old woman but not feeling any pain. She shuffled over and stood in front of the boy.

"How come YOU'RE still young and I'M old!" 90 year old Ashley demanded of 11 year old Cody, planting her hands on her thick hips of the flannel nightgown she'd died in.

"Hello to you too, Ash," Cody laughed and jumped forward excitedly to give her a big hug. "Don't worry," he said, pointing at her body, "you'll be back to your old self in no time. C'mon!"

He grabbed her hand and led her past the gathered crowd of loved ones. She spotted her parents in the back of the crowd.

"Hold on..." she told Cody, slowing down, but Cody grabbed her hand tighter and practically dragged her forward.

"Don't worry, there will be time later."

He was pulling her forward deeper and deeper into the clouds, which swirled around like white cotton candy at their knees. Finally, they ended up at - *of course!* - a basketball court. It was the biggest and most perfect basketball court she'd ever seen, complete with a little garden bench over in the corner. The bench was an exact replica of the one from her driveway in the house she'd grown up in. The clay was perfect, the paint, perfection, with crisp colors, sharp lines and, of course, a Chicago Bulls logo smack dab in the center of the court.

She should have been excited but instead Ashley was a little disappointed. She looked down at her old body. She was grateful for the family it had produced, but now she felt only frustrated. This body had done its job. It was time for something new...

Meanwhile Cody was already on the court, dribbling up and down like a pro. He seemed to have gotten even better than he was on earth.

"Coh... I can't..." Ashley said sadly, pointing down at her body.

"CAN'T? Miss Ashley saying - can't? I never thought I'd see the day!" Cody teased, dancing around the court lightly on his sneakered feet.

"Well now you're just being mean," she snapped, sounding very much like he remembered her.

"Heads up!" Cody suddenly exclaimed and fired the ball at the sideline. Ashley's wrinkled arms instinctively flew up and she caught the ball perfectly, even though it had been decades since she'd done so.

"See?" Cody confirmed with a mischievous grin.

Ashley rolled the ball around in her hands, thinking. Then, cautiously, she slid one slipper-clad foot onto the rust-colored clay. And then - miraculously - the slipper turned into a Bulls-red pair of Air Jordans. She kept walking forward until...

"Ah-HA! There you are again!" Cody exclaimed joyfully.

Ashley looked down and sure enough she was 11 years old again. She smiled tearily at Cody.

"Hi," she said, sniffling.

"Hi," he said back, still beaming.

She continued to stand there, taking it all in.

"Okay, you gonna cry or play ball?" Cody said with a wink. "The point is the game Ash - always has been. You know that."

Ashley wiped her eyes, nodded, put her game face on, and began driving toward the hoop.

It was good to be home.

***

"Any luck yet?" Michael called across the attic to his college-aged daughter Amanda.

Ashley's son Michael was a fashionably middle-aged cool dad- at least that's what he liked to think, having inherited a healthy dose of self confidence from his mom. His daughter Amanda was home for the weekend from Stanford, where she was currently at the top of her class in engineering.

"Nope, not yet," Amanda said, her back to him as she ducked her head and walked over to the final corner of her grandma's attic, stacked high with yet more boxes.

Michael gingerly unfolded his long legs and stood up only partially to avoid whacking his head on the low wood beams, and shook some feeling back into the lower half of his body. He and Amanda had been up there for hours sorting through frail dusty boxes of his mom's things, on the hunt for a mystery box of "very special Christmas ornaments" Ashley had told them about as she lay dying in her bed. Amanda had to restrain herself from running right up to the attic right then and start searching for the box.

Christmas was her absolute favorite holiday ever. Amanda was one of those people that, to the annoyance of the "non-Christmas-y" people, began her holiday shopping in July and then counted down to the earliest possible "acceptable" day to put up Christmas decorations (she never did make it to Thanksgiving).

So, when her grandmother told her about this box of "very special Christmas ornaments", Amanda couldn't wait to begin the search with her dad. The most curious thing they'd uncovered so far, however, was a shoebox full of old ticket stubs to the planetarium at the old Chicago Science Museum, which was now an online shopping warehouse. Neither of them understood the significance but both were sure that, knowing Ashley, there was a fascinating story attached to those faded stubs.

But, just as father and daughter were sure they'd covered every square inch of the attic…

"Omigod, I think I found it!!!" Amanda squealed, sounding the way she had as a little girl, seeing the presents under the tree first thing on Christmas morning.

"Good girl!" Michael said. He smiled as he ducked under beams and squat-walked his way into the corner of the attic where Amanda was kneeling in front of a medium-sized box.

The corners of the box looked like something had been nibbling on them. The box itself was sitting in a circle of faded glitter and flakes of dried up glue that had spilled through the corner holes. Michael wondered how he'd never noticed it before, especially with the glitter circle around it. Amanda carefully removed the thin and mostly cracked pieces of scotch tape holding the top flaps together, and opened it.

"Oh, wow... dad..." she whispered in awe as she saw what was inside.

Her dad peeked over her shoulder into the box. It looked like a craft store had blown up. Glitter, satin ribbons, specks of dried glue, and all colors of tissue paper and construction paper lined the bottom of the box. But the most incredible part was what was piled high in the middle - Styrofoam bells. By now the bells were only partially decorated, with the rest of their adornments making up the mess on the box floor. Even so, it was clear to see what they had once been and who had made them, the artists' names scrawled on each one.

Katie, age 6.

Dwayne, age 8,

Maria, grade 2.

There were dozens of them and each bell had a satin ribbon looped through the top of it, perfect for attaching to a Christmas ornament hook.

Michael instantly realized - *These were the Heaven's Bells made by mom's students over the years!*

He made eye contact with his daughter and, pretending not to see the tears welling up in her eyes, went back to looking through the box. Then he spotted a photo of Ashley standing proudly with her first grade class. He looked at the date on the back - it was from back in 2034. That would make his mom around, he calculated quickly in his head, 25, a few years older than Amanda was now. He picked up the photo and examined it and then looked over the top at his daughter.

"Wow, can you BE any more like your grandma?" her dad teased.

"Stop it dad!"

"What?" Michael asked innocently.

"Stop comparing me to grandma again," Amanda said, gathering her blonde hair into a ponytail as she continued sifting through the bells.

"You literally look like all the photos I've ever seen of her including this one," Michael said, holding up the class photo, "except for your mom's hair, of course. Why is that a problem?"

"It's not," Amanda said, taking the photo from him, studying it for a moment. Then she put the photo carefully back into the book and stared at her dad with a strong look, "But that was her - I'm me."

Michael had to admit she was right. Amanda was definitely her own person and nobody was going to convince her otherwise.

He slung an arm around his daughter. "You 100% are. But you're also forever connected to grandma - you're a part of her and she's a part of you."

Amanda picked up one of the Styrofoam bells (*"Asia, 3rd Grade"*), spinning it around in her perfectly manicured hands.

"I miss her," she said. "Me too," her dad said, "but you know what that means…"

"Yeah, yeah dad," Amanda said, taping the top flaps of the box together, picking it up, and walking toward the attic steps with it in tow. "I think it's safe to say I know the story of Heaven's Bell by now!"

"Then you know what's happening up there now," Michael said as he cast his eyes up toward the attic beams.

It had been less than a week since the funeral and they were still feeling Ashley's absence. Even as an old woman, she was still a big personality.

Amanda followed his gaze upward, then lowered her eyes again and looked straight at her dad with a focus and intensity that even her grandma never showed.

"I want to make her proud," Amanda said firmly.

"You already have, honey."

"Let's go get these bells hung on the tree then!" Amanda said, her blue eyes sparkling.

***

Meanwhile, up in heaven, Ashley was on the court as usual, playing ball with Cody and a few other new friends. One of those new friends, as it turned out, was also family. Ashley tossed the basketball over Cody's no longer thinning head of black hair to a boy their age with curly sandy brown hair that tended to collect sweat easily - hair that never seemed to behave itself.

"Thanks sis!" the boy exclaimed and made a perfect shot.

From across the court, Ashley air high fived the brother who had never made it from her mom's tummy into the real world.

"Oh great, now there's TWO of her!" Cody exclaimed playfully to the group as he snatched up the ball and began dribbling.

"That's right, Coh. Twice the dunking, nothing but net, half court shot awesomeness my friend," Ashley said, doing a victory dance center court, still celebrating her restored 11 year old athletic body.

"Okay, okay, what's the score?" Cody asked, then quickly added, "And don't lie!"

"Actually, I don't think we're allowed to up here," Ashley laughed.

She started to mentally tally the score, but as soon as she heard her Heaven's Bell ring, she quickly made the time out sign, and ran off the court. Minutes later, she was sprinting up the Great Hall, LOVING her young new body again, toward the Bell Room. She ran until she finally found her bell and planted herself underneath it, staring up in wonder at its incredible beauty.

As it rang, back and forth, over and over and over, she thought back on her life and all the people in it. Some were up here with her in "outer space", and others, like Michael and Amanda, were still down on earth, undoubtedly being the ones who were making the bell ring now. Even though they were temporarily separated by this infinite distance, the moments they'd shared kept them at arm's length.

Ashley smiled, thinking of the day that would eventually come when she, Cody, Michael and Amanda would all be able to play basketball together up here.

As she jogged back down the Great Hall toward the game in progress, she mentally began figuring out teams for the future game. Girls against boys, she decided.

We'll kick their butts!

Ashley grinned as she exited the Great Hall, sprinting through the knee deep clouds, excited to tell Cody her plan.

The End

Conclusion:
"Your Heaven's Bell"

It was a peaceful, summer evening at the Castle Rock Lake cabin in Arkdale Wisconsin, when I first wrote something I titled "Your Heaven's Bell," the same words that inspired the story you've just read.

It was the summer of 2016. Sitting out on the screened-in patio watching dainty ripples dance across the water, the quietness enveloping me was significant. I've always heard from people that when they lose a loved one it's hardest when it's quiet and they are alone with their sorrow. Then, over time, that sorrow left in death's wake is transformed into memories by those left behind about their loved ones in heaven.

The idea of bells ringing to signify those thoughts began when I was in grade school when I first imagined bells ringing to let my loved ones know whenever I was thinking of them. It started as all my loved ones, earthbound and separated by distance, as well as ones who had passed. My theory of the bells helped me not miss them as much because I felt I could still share my memories and love with them by mentally ringing their bell. I pictured them listening and smiling at the memories that made their bell ring.

In 2012, I first shared my story of bells, particularly bells in heaven, with my young nieces who lost their grandma. Immediately upon hearing my story, the girls opened up and began eagerly sharing their memories and stories about their grandma, including what they thought grandma was doing "up in heaven".

From that point on, I began sharing the story with all I felt who needed to hear it. It soon became a safe conversation starter for children and adults alike, especially when the loss was fresh and the emotional wounds still open. Each age group was just as impacted as the other when hearing about "the bells", shedding tears and enthusiastically letting memories and stories about their loved ones spill forth. Each telling of my (still solely verbal) story about "the heaven's bells" inevitably ended with hugs all around and more peace than was there before.

So, on that lovely summer evening in 2016, when I spotted a large "cabin journal" left for me by the owner, my soul told me exactly which words needed to go on those pages. It was finally time, after all these years, to put this story I'd been telling, this story that brought so much comfort to so many people, young and old, down onto paper. On that quiet June evening looking out on the lake, it took me less than 10 minutes to write out my story.

Your Heaven's Bell
(Original Story)

Do you know what happens when our loved ones die and go to heaven? Well, they open their eyes and see bright beautiful bells and hear hundreds maybe even thousands ringing. Heaven's Bells are ringing and welcoming your loved one to heaven. And your loved one is smiling and so happy to be in heaven surrounded by beautiful bells and the music they make together.

And as you and each one of their loved ones down on earth say goodbye, a bell is hung in heaven. And guess what? Did you know that every time we think about our loved one their bell rings? It does. Your bell has its own special ring. Your loved one will always know you are thinking of them and sending your love when they hear your Heaven's Bell ringing.

Each ringing bell represents one special relationship on earth. Each bell in your loved one's cozy place in heaven represents someone they may have helped, showed kindness toward or loved - a life they touched. These relationships and memories keep the bells ringing.

As the years go by, one by one, the bells slowly stop ringing. As the bells become old, worn out and silent, our loved one in heaven becomes more and more excited! Yes, excited! You see, when all their bells in heaven stop ringing, it's because all of you are together again - in heaven! It's a big celebration in heaven that day with dancing and singing and probably cake, too.

Think about the bells you are creating all the time, everyday! Maybe you create a beautiful bell for a neighbor when you help them or for your friend who is sad and needs your help. Your acts of kindness and every relationship you develop will create bells for you and your special loved ones. Creating your Heaven's Bells gives happiness here on earth and makes music in heaven.

Go find opportunities to create your bells and think of your loved ones often so you can ring all those Heaven's Bells already hung in heaven!

About
Sherrie Barch

"Legacy is built not by what we achieve,
but through those we inspire to achieve."

Sherrie Barch is the CEO of two Forbes' ranked top executive search firms and a leadership consulting company. An expert in the areas of leadership, team development, and diversity, her forward-thinking approach to work was recognized when she was chosen to participate in the "altMBA" program designed and led by leadership guru Seth Godin. Born and raised in Northern Illinois, Sherrie earned B.A. and M.A. degrees in Communication from Western Illinois University.

Sherrie is married with three sons. As a mom, she describes herself as a part-time pancreas for her two youngest sons who were both diagnosed with Type 1 Diabetes within the same year. Playing this role for the last 11 years, she is relentless about creating open and honest communication with her family about this chronic and life-threatening condition.

Sherrie's passion for storytelling and making room for serious and "heavy" conversations was a strong motivation for her to write her children's book *Heaven's Bell* based on a story of the same name she penned several years prior. The story focuses on 11-year-old best friends Cody and Ashley, and what happens when their once-in-a-lifetime friendship is threatened by personal tragedy. One of her goals for *Heaven's Bell* is to create and inspire a safe space for families to have a conversation about death and dying in a natural and productive way.

Sherrie is currently working on her second book, a business leadership fable designed to help new college graduates navigate the "real life stuff they don't teach you in school" about career conversations, conflicts, and challenges.

In her leisure time, she enjoys the changing seasons of the Midwest, spending time with her family and friends and live entertainment in any form including Broadway plays, school plays, comedians, magicians, and musicians.

> To contact the author please email
> sherrie@sherriebarch.com.
>
> For updates, merchandise, and other items
> related to Heaven's Bell, please visit
> www.heavensbell.com.

Bibliography

Brennan, Dan, ed. "How Might Children React Sometimes to Heavy Conversations about Their Life-Threatening Condition?" WebMD. WebMD, January 14, 2020. https://www.webmd.com/palliative-care/qa/how-might-children-react-sometimes-to-heavy-conversations-about-their-lifethreatening-condition.

"Talking to Children about Death." WebMD. WebMD, January 14, 2020. https://www.webmd.com/palliative-care/talking_to_children_about_death.

"Helping Grieving Children and Teenagers." Cancer.Net. American Society of Clinical Oncology. March 20, 2018. https://www.cancer.net/coping-with-cancer/managing-emotions/grief-and-loss/helping-grieving-children-and-teenagers.

Memories

Memories

Memories

Memories

Memories

Memories

Memories

Memories

Made in the USA
Columbia, SC
25 April 2021